12.95

B&T.

4/91

GRANDPA CLAUS

by Brian Pilkington

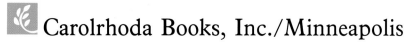 Carolrhoda Books, Inc./Minneapolis

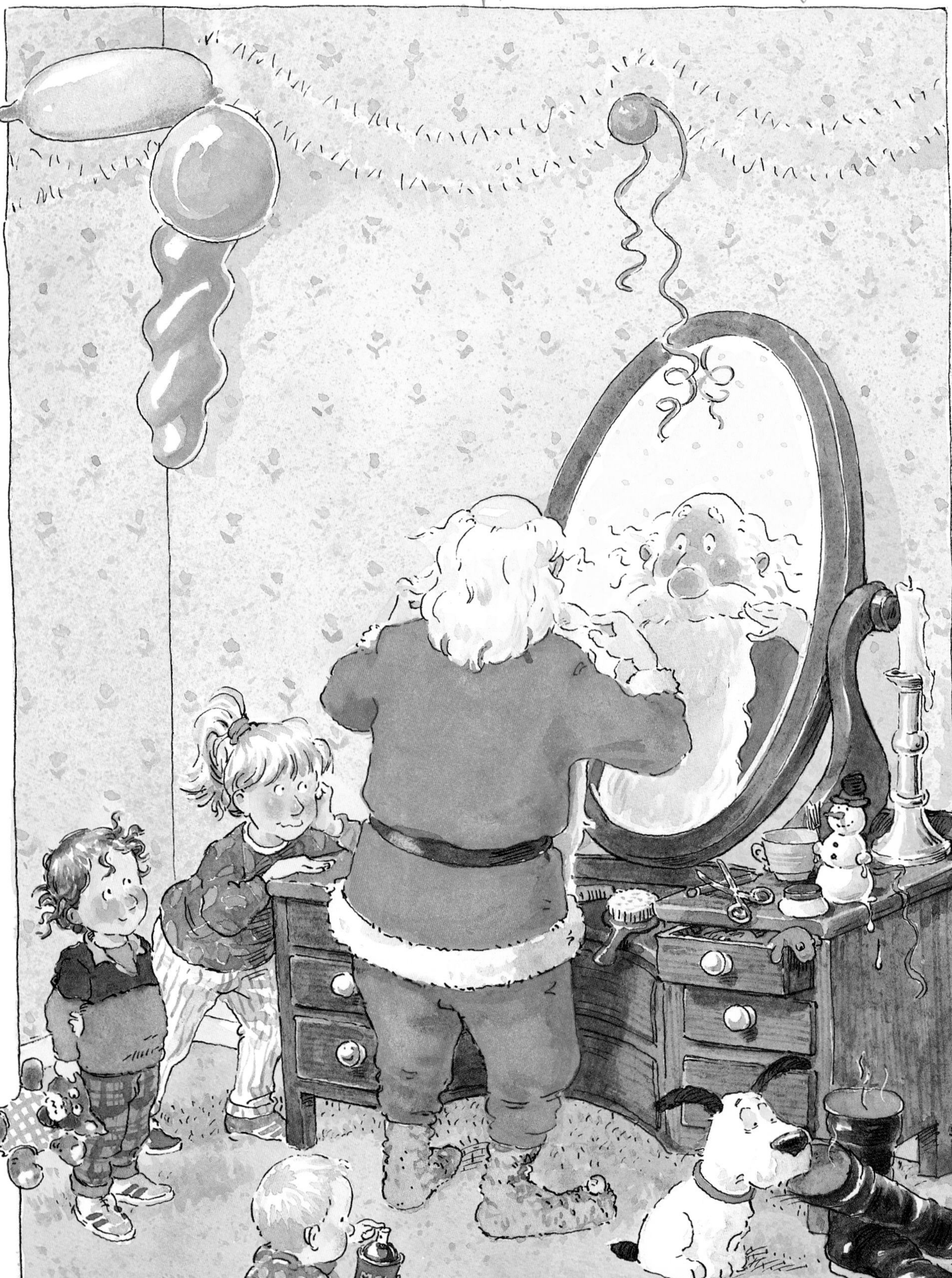

This plump gentleman with the beautiful white beard, who we see here putting on his red uniform, is one of the nicest fellows you could hope to meet. Everybody knows that Santa Claus is the friendliest and kindest of people, of course.

Ah! But this isn't the real Santa Claus. This is Harry, the man our story is about.

We all know that not everyone who dresses in a red suit and has a long white beard is the real thing. Most, in fact, don't look anything like Santa Claus. Their cheap fake beards don't fool anybody. But Harry is really good — he looks just like Santa. He may be the best Santa impersonator there has ever been. Harry's beard is real, too. He's been growing it for years and years and has become quite attached to it. He tells his grandchildren that he was born with a beard. But he's probably only joking!

SOME
NOT VERY
CONVINCING
SANTAS

Harry's job is an unusual one. He gets the sack as soon as he starts work! Usually when people say they got the sack, they mean that they were fired. But Harry gets a real sack—full of toys!

For five or six weeks before Christmas, Harry is very busy. He sometimes works from nine o'clock in the morning until ten o'clock at night. He visits schools and is invited to parties. He also works for a large department store, walking around inside and outside, generally cheering people up and getting them into a Christmassy mood.

Most of his time, though, is taken up at the mall. Long, long lines of noisy, sticky children come to say hello to him. They're usually tired and grumpy from walking around the mall all afternoon. But they always cheer up when they see Harry, and he's always pleased to see them. Many of them bring lists of things they want for Christmas. Harry always makes sure the real Santa Claus gets the lists.

The children also like to have their pictures taken with
Harry, and he gives each one a small present to take home.
There's nothing in the world Harry loves more than
playing Santa!

Christmas day is the happiest and most special day of the year for many people, and so it is for Harry's family. They all get together for a BIG Christmas dinner. Everybody has a wonderful time opening their presents, singing Christmas carols, playing games, and eating and drinking as much as they can.

Harry is very popular with the children because he keeps on his red suit at the table. There aren't many children who have a Santa Claus at their own Christmas dinner!

Christmas doesn't last forever, though, and the days right after Christmas are sad ones for Harry. There's no more suspense or excitement for him. After weeks of waiting, all the presents have been opened, all the carols sung, and all the mince pies eaten. There is nothing more to look forward to. And poor Harry is out of a job!

Nobody needs a Santa Claus once Christmas is over. Harry is no longer the center of attention—and having nothing to do makes him feel sad and unwanted. The worst thing for Harry is having to put away his red suit. Next Christmas is 364 days away! A whole year!

But there's one thing Harry can't put away after Christmas —his magnificent beard!

He can't shave it off because it would take years to grow that long again. And he'll need it for next Christmas, of course!

Taking care of his beard is a lot of work. He doesn't always like getting it wet because it takes such a long time to dry. He even has his own specially designed shower cap.

But when he does wash his beard it's quite a ceremony, since he wants it to look as splendid as possible!

Harry can't spend all day taking care of his beard, however, and having so little to do bothers him quite a bit. He manages to fill in some of his time by making himself useful around the house. But even the simplest household jobs have their problems!

Harry lives with his grandchildren and their parents, and so he spends some of his time looking after the children. He takes Jessica to daycare on his bike.

She is very considerate and always helps her grandpa up hills by pushing from behind.

Harry often passes the time by taking baby Simon out for a walk in his stroller. He likes playing hide-and-seek with Clare and her friends. Harry is good at the seeking part, but hiding isn't always so easy!

Even with the children to care for, Harry still has time on his hands. He begins looking for a job to keep him busy. In early spring, at long last, he's lucky enough to find himself a job at a hotel.

Spring can often be a very trying time for people with long beards, especially when birds are collecting material for their nests.

And his new job presents him with a whole pile of new problems!

Doors have always been difficult, of course.

Car doors, he discovers,
are even worse!
　But elevators—oh, boy!!
　Elevators are a nightmare!!

After a series of accidents,
Harry gives up his job at the
hotel.　He even goes around
for a while with his beard
tucked safely into his sweater.

Spring is soon over, and Christmas is getting closer. But even in the summer sunshine, Harry doesn't feel at ease. He'd much rather be busy than lying out in the sun. But—"If a job's worth doing, it's worth doing well!" Harry always says!

Later in the summer, Harry manages to get a job entertaining children in the local park. He's really pleased with himself. This will keep him busy, and he'll be with children and be the center of attention again!

But the job isn't as easy as Harry imagined it would be. Selling cotton candy turns out to be more difficult than he expected. And as for his one-man band! Well, he certainly gets lots of requests — mostly to play somewhere else! Poor old Harry! If only there were three or four Christmases throughout the year!

Harry loses his job at the park when summer vacation is over and the children return to school. But as fall goes on, Harry begins to look forward once more to Christmas.

On your mark

Get set

GO!

Ho!!

He knows he has to stay fit to keep up with all the long hours ahead in the mall and at parties. So he begins to run and skip around the neighborhood.

He even tries going to ballet classes in the evenings, but he soon finds out that ballet is not for him! He gets most of his exercise playing on the senior citizens' soccer team. He plays "Santa" forward, of course!

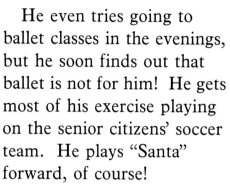

Santa forward

Right Winger

At last, toward the middle of November, the Christmas season starts down at the mall. Harry is always the first to arrive there, and he's always ready to help out. He helps hang up Christmas lights all over the mall, and wreaths and tinsel everywhere.

Instead of a single Christmas tree, there is one at each end of the mall—and a few in the window displays, too.

All this is hard work, but you won't hear Harry complain. For him this is the best possible way to have fun. He works twice as hard as anyone else. In fact, he sometimes gets so carried away when he's finished with the Christmas trees that he starts to decorate himself!

When all the decorations are up and Harry has had a chance to catch his breath, the big moment arrives. He gets the sack again! The sack that's full of toys, of course. He puts on his red suit and black boots, then he combs his beard.

Harry is Santa Claus once more!

As Christmas approaches, Harry is the happiest man in the world, bubbling over with delight. At last he's doing the thing he does best!

So the next time you see a man with a red coat, black boots, and a beautiful long white beard, be very kind and polite to him. Because you never know, it might be the *real* Santa Claus! Or even better—it might be Harry!

This edition first published 1990 by Carolrhoda Books, Inc.
First published in Iceland in 1990 by Idunn under the title AFI
GAMLI JOLASVEINN.
Copyright ©1990 by Brian Pilkington

English language rights arranged by Kerstin Kvint Literary and
Co-Production Agency, Stockholm, Sweden.

LIBRARY OF CONGRESS CATALOGING-IN-PUBLICATION DATA

Pilkington, Brian.
  Grandpa Claus/by Brian Pilkington.
    p. cm.
  Originally published under title: Afi Gamli Jolasveinn.
  Summary: When it's not Christmas, Harry, a man who plays Santa
Claus at a mall, feels a little out of it.
  [1. Santa Claus — Fiction. 2. Christmas — Fiction. 3. Old age —
Fiction.] I. Title.
PZ7.P63125Gr 1990   90-32476
[E] — dc20   CIP
                                                          AC

Manufactured in the United States of America

1 2 3 4 5 6 7 8 9 10 99 98 97 96 95 94 93 92 91 90